PIPPA POPS OUT!

OTHER YEARLING BOOKS YOU WILL ENJOY:

Pippa Mouse, BETTY BOEGEHOLD
Here's Pippa Again!, BETTY BOEGEHOLD
Dorrie and the Blue Witch, PATRICIA COOMBS
Dorrie and the Haunted House, PATRICIA COOMBS
Lisa and the Grompet, PATRICIA COOMBS
A Toad for Tuesday, RUSSELL E. ERICKSON
Warton and Morton, RUSSELL E. ERICKSON
Warton's Christmas Eve Adventure, RUSSELL E. ERICKSON
The Beetle Bush, BEVERLY KELLER
Fiona's Bee, BEVERLY KELLER

YEARLING BOOKS are designed especially to entertain and enlighten young people. The finest available books for children have been selected under the direction of Charles F. Reasoner, Professor of Elementary Education, New York University.

For a complete listing of all Yearling titles, write to Education Sales Department, Dell Publishing Co., Inc., 1 Dag Hammarskjold Plaza, New York, N.Y. 10017.

PIPPA POPS OUT!

by Betty Boegehold
Illustrated by Cyndy Szekeres

A Yearling Book

TO KAREN SMITH
—with love and thanks
for being my most supportive critic.

Published by
Dell Publishing Co., Inc.
1 Dag Hammarskjold Plaza
New York, New York 10017

Yearling ® TM 913705, Dell Publishing Co., Inc.

ISBN: 0-440-46865-5

Reprinted by arrangement with Alfred A. Knopf, Inc.

Printed in the United States of America

First Yearling printing—September 1980
CW

The Stories

The Moony Night

Pippa Mouse peeks out
of the mouse-house door.
"Cricket," she says.
"It's a moony summer night.
Come out and play."

"All right," says her pet, Cricket,
"for summer nights are cricket nights."

Father Mouse asks, "Pippa,
are you big enough
to play outside
on a moon-light night?"

"Yes," says Pippa.
"I'm big enough
and old enough
so I will go out."

"Stay safe," says Father Mouse.

Outside, Pippa and Cricket jump around
making long moon shadows.
"Look at my monster shadow," yells Pippa.
"I'm a Moon Monster,
a Moon Monster Mouse!"
"And I'm a Mars Monster," calls Cricket.
"See my big feelers waving all around."
Pippa stops jumping.
"Cricket," she says,
"in the moonlight,
you are not green anymore.
You are the color of water.
You are no color at all."
"Well, you are a ghost color, too,"
says Cricket.
"You are a Moon Monster Ghost, Pippa."

"I don't want to play
Ghosts and Monsters any longer,"
says Pippa.
"I want to play Hide-and-Seek.
I will hide, and you will seek.
Count to 10, Cricket.
Then come find me."

"All right," says Cricket.
He puts his feelers over his eyes and counts.
"One ... two ... four ... three ... six. ..."
Pippa runs off to hide.

"I will hide under the toadstool," says Pippa.
But where is the toadstool?
Everything looks very strange
in the moony night,
and the toadstool is lost in shadows.

"Is this just a dark shadow?" asks Pippa.
Bump!
"No, this is a big stone," says Pippa,
rubbing her nose.
"But I will hide right here
in the shadow of this big stone."

Pippa creeps into the stone's shadow
and stays very still.

The black and silver trees are quiet,
and the black shadows are quiet, too.
"Are those shadows moving?"
Pippa asks herself.
She squeezes tight against the stone
and holds her breath.

All is quiet. Very very quiet.
"Cricket, where are you?"
Pippa whispers.
"Come find me right away, Cricket."

Cricket doesn't come,
but something else does.
Some little green-light thing
blinking on and off in the dark.

In a very small voice, Pippa asks,
"Are those green monster eyes
blinking on and off?"
And a very small voice answers,
"Silly Pippa! I am not a monster.
I am a firefly dancing in the night."

Then all around Pippa
little lights are blinking on and off,
off and on.
"Come dance with us, Pippa,"
the fireflies call
as they drift away in the dark.

But Pippa stays still,
very still under the stone,
for something else is floating down,
floating down without a sound.
Is it Owl drifting down without a sound?
Pippa squeezes tighter against the stone
and stays very still.
Then the floating something
lands by the stone
and Pippa sees
that it is only a leaf.
A silver leaf from a silver tree
floating to the ground.

Pippa gives herself a shake
and pops out from under the stone.
"If Cricket can't find me," she says,
"then I will find him.
I will find him right away."
She starts to run, then stops.
"Which way?" says Pippa.
"Which way did I come?
By that black bush
or by that tall silver tree?"

In the silver and shadow night
everything looks clear but strange.
Pippa sits and thinks.
She thinks very hard.

"When I came here," says Pippa,
"the moon was on my nose.
So if I turn all the way around,
the moon will be on my tail.
And if I keep the moon on my tail,
I will find my way home."

Pippa runs off with the moon on her tail,
in and out of the shadows,
under the black and silver trees,
right to her mouse house.

There is Cricket,
singing a cricket song
in the white moon light.
"Cricket, I found you!" yells Pippa.

"Oh," says Cricket. "Was I lost?"

Father Mouse is there, too.
"Cricket looked for you, Pippa,"
says Father Mouse.

"But you weren't there
—not anywhere there."
says Father Mouse.

"Oh yes, I was there," says Pippa.
"And now I am here.
For I am old enough
—and big enough
—and smart enough
to find my way home
on a dark and moony night."

17

The Nothing-Mouse

Pippa and her friends
are down by the lake
They are telling each other
how good they are.

"My tail is very long," says Pippa.

"But mine is longer," says Ripple Squirrel,
"and it's much, much fluffier.
And I can jump higher than you can."

"Well," says Gray Bird, "I can fly.
And I can sing better than anyone."

"I'm a good swimmer," says Pippa.

"But I'm better," says Weber Duck.
"Much, much better than you, Pippa Mouse."

"I don't want to stay here anymore,"
says Pippa.
"I'm going home."
Pippa goes home,
dragging her tail.

Cricket is sitting in the sun
by the mouse-house door.
"What is the matter, Pippa?"
he asks.

"Nothing," says Pippa.

"Oh," says Cricket.
"Is nothing
why your head is down
and your tail
is dragging on the ground?"

"I am a nothing-mouse," says Pippa.
"I don't have a fluffy tail like Ripple,
I can't sing like Gray Bird,
or swim like Weber Duck.
I can't jump as high as you can, Cricket,
or even make your crickety sound
in the night."

"Why should you?" asks Cricket.
"You are not a duck or a bird.
You are not a squirrel
or even a cricket.
You are a mouse,
a just-right mouse."

"No, no," says Pippa.
"I am a nothing-mouse."

"Wrong," says Cricket.
"You are not a nothing-mouse.
Right now, you are
a very-sorry-for-yourself mouse."

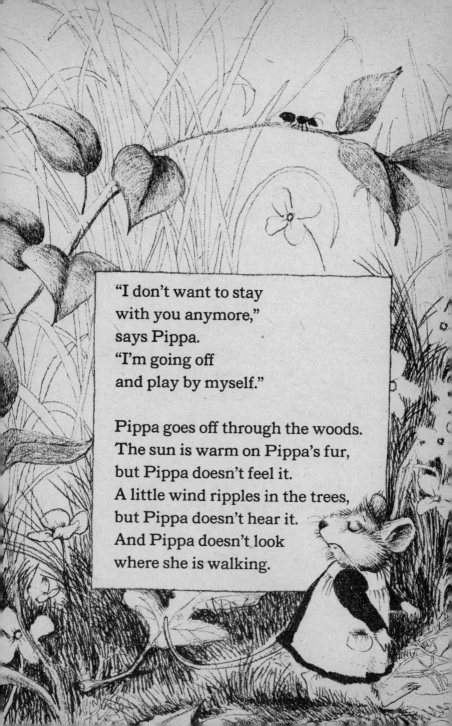

"I don't want to stay
with you anymore,"
says Pippa.
"I'm going off
and play by myself."

Pippa goes off through the woods.
The sun is warm on Pippa's fur,
but Pippa doesn't feel it.
A little wind ripples in the trees,
but Pippa doesn't hear it.
And Pippa doesn't look
where she is walking.

Bump!
Pippa bumps
into something large and black.
The something is Big Beetle,
lying on his back,
kicking his six black legs in the air.
"Help! Help!" calls Big Beetle.

"I'll help turn you over,"
says Pippa quickly.
She pushes and pulls
and tugs and shoves
with all her mouse muscles.
Big Beetle kicks and kicks
and wiggles and wiggles.
Then—plop!
Big Beetle is turned over.
"Thank you, Pippa," says Big Beetle.
"You are a mighty strong mouse."

"Yes," says Pippa.
"I am a mighty strong mouse.
Goodby, Big Beetle."

Big Beetle goes one way
and Pippa goes the other.
She picks up a little pebble
and throws it against a tree.

"I'm a mighty good pebble throw-er, too,"
says Pippa.
Now she begins to run through the woods,
jumping over sticks and stones.
The little wind is cool
on her warm fur.

25

As Pippa comes down to the lake again,
Weber, Ripple and Gray Bird
are playing tag.

"Hi, Pippa," says Gray Bird.
"We are playing tag.
Do you want to be *It*?"

"Sure," says Pippa.

First, Pippa tags Weber.
Then she tags Ripple.
And then she catches Gray Bird.
"I'm a mighty fine catcher!"
yells Pippa.

Then someone says
"I'm a good catcher, too.
A very good catcher."

The someone is Black Cat.

Black Cat blinks her green eyes and says,
"I will play tag, too. I will be *It*.
And I will catch you, Pippa Mouse."

PZZZZZZ-ZIP!—SPLASH!
Weber jumps into the water,
Gray Bird flies up into a tree,
and Ripple scolds from a branch.

But where is Pippa?
She is deep in a hole under a stone.

Black Cat sits on the stone,
blinking her green eyes.
"Come out, come out," she says.
"Come out, wherever you are.
You are not playing fair, Pippa.
I can't even see you."

But Pippa doesn't come out,
and Pippa doesn't say a word.
After a bit, Black Cat yawns
and jumps down from the stone.
"All right for you, Pippa Mouse.
If you won't play fair," says Black Cat,
"I won't play with you at all.
I'm going home."
Away goes Black Cat
waving the tip of her tail.

Gray Bird flies back,
Ripple jumps down,
and Weber comes out of the water.

"We can't see you either, Pippa,"
calls Ripple.
"You are a very good hider," says Gray Bird.
"Come out, come out, wherever you are,"
calls Weber.

Pip-Pop. Pippa pops out.
"I'm a no-more nothing-mouse,"
says Pippa.
"I'm a good hider
and runner and jumper.
And I'm a very good
turner-over of beetles."

Then she looks at the woods
where Black Cat has gone.
"And I am
a smarter-than-a-cat mouse, too,"
says Pippa.

Flying Pippa

A wild March wind is blowing.
Old leaves are chasing one another.
Bits of paper, dust, and dead twigs
dance in the air.
Pippa's cap flies away.

"I want to fly, too," says Pippa,
running after her cap.
"I want to sail on the wind."

Gray Bird is soaring over Pippa's head.
"Gray Bird, how do you fly?" calls Pippa.

"You lean on the wind
and flap your wings," calls Gray Bird.

Gray Bird leans on the wind
and flaps her wings
and sails away over the trees.

32

"I will do that, too," says Pippa.

She climbs on a rock.
She leans on the wind
and flaps all her paws.
Bump.
Down comes Pippa.

"I need wings, not paws," says Pippa.
She finds two dry leaves.
She holds one in each paw
and takes a running jump off the rock.

Flap, flap, flop.
Down comes Pippa.

"Silly mouse," says someone.
Ripple Squirrel is sitting on a branch
with her tail blowing over her head.
"Poor Pippa," she says.
"The wind blows you down.
But the wind helps me jump.
Watch!"

Ripple Squirrel leaps into the air,
her tail streaming into the wind.
She leaps from branch to branch.

"My tail is a sail," calls Ripple.

"I will sail from rock to rock,"
says Pippa.
She leaps from her rock.
Bump.
Pippa lands on the ground.
"My tail is more like a string,"
says Pippa.
"If I do not have wings
or a sail tail,
then I will make
a real sail."

Pippa runs home
to her mouse-hole house.
She takes some nails,
some string,
and a rock.
She takes a leaf sheet from her bed.

"Are you sleeping outside?"
asks Cricket.
"No, I am hang-gliding outside,"
says Pippa.
"I will sail on the wind
and fly in the air.
Want to fly in the air with me?"

"Not I," says Cricket.
"Crickets are jumpers,
not flyers."

"Then please help me find
some strong twigs," says Pippa.
Bang, bang, bang.
Pippa nails the strong twigs
and the string to the sheet.

"Now watch me glide
in my hang-glider,"
says Pippa.
She climbs up on a tall rock.
She runs and jumps into the air.

"See me hang-gliding!"
yells Pippa.

The wind blows the hang-glider
high in the air
with Pippa hanging below.

Pippa calls,
"See the mouse sailing in air!
Look up and see!
Hang-gliding Pippa, that's me!"

Now the hang-glider
starts to slip down the air.
It slips and it slides
down into an old apple tree.
And there is Pippa
hanging free.

"Now I'm swinging," says Pippa.
"See me swinging
high in the old apple tree."

Red Fox comes by.
"What is that I see?" he asks.
"Is that a fat little bat
in the old apple tree?
Or a mouse swinging high
in the sky?"

Red Fox sits down
and curls his tail around his paws.
"If I wait," says Red Fox,
"that funny little mouse-bat
will come down right here.
And I will find out who she is."

Pippa holds onto the glider,
and the hang-glider begins to slip
slowly, slowly
from the branch of the old apple tree.

"I'll climb up the string,"
says Pippa.
But the string is too skinny
and Pippa's paws slip and slide.

"Oh, my paws and whiskers!"
says Pippa.
"Red Fox won't have
to wait very long,
for I think I am going down
to the ground very soon."

"No, no," says Ripple Squirrel
in the branch above Pippa.
"You are not going *down*.
You are coming *up*."

Paw over paw, Ripple pulls Pippa
up to the apple tree branch.

Down on the ground,
Red Fox trots away, saying,
"I'm much too busy
to play with mice today."

Pippa and Ripple are safe,
high in the old apple tree.

"Thank you, Ripple," says Pippa.
"Every mouse needs a helping friend."

Pippa-Squeak's Surprise

Pippa finds her friends
down by the lake.

"Look at Pippa," says Weber Duck.

Pippa is wearing a long cape
and a black hat.
Cricket has a pointy hat with stars.

"Why are you all dressed up?"
asks Gray Bird.
"What are you, Pippa?"
asks Ripple Squirrel.
"Are you Mouse Dracula?"

"No, no," says Pippa.
"I am Pippa-Squeak, the Magic Mouse,
and here is my first trick."

She takes off her black hat.
"See, my hat is empty," she says.

"No, it isn't," says Ripple.
"There's a paper sticking out of it."

"Wait a minute," says Pippa.
She turns her back to her friends
and reaches into her hat.
Then she tucks something under her arm
and turns around.

"Now my hat is empty,"
says Pippa.

Ripple says,
"But now there's a paper under . . ."

"Don't talk so much, Ripple.
It isn't polite to talk
when someone is doing a magic trick,"
says Pippa.

She turns her back again and
reaches under her arm.
She puts something into her hat
and turns around.

"Ta-*da*!" yells Pippa.
"See what Pippa-Squeak, the Magic Mouse,
has found in her magic hat!"
She pulls out a piece of paper
with words on it.

COME
to a party at
the house of
Pippa-Squeak
the Magic Mouse

"What's so magic about that?"
asks Gray Bird.

"Will we get something to eat?"
asks Weber Duck.

"Sure," says Pippa-Squeak.
"Parties always have eats."

"Then let's go," says Ripple Squirrel.

Mother Mouse opens the door.
"Come in," she says.
"Shall we eat right away?"

"Eat! Eat!" says Weber Duck.

"Good," says Father Mouse.
"For I am very hungry."

Everyone sits down at the big table.
"Look!" shouts Pippa. "We are eating
Magic Mouse Food!
Carrot-and-cheese witch hats
and scary-face apples!"

Everyone eats and eats
until even Weber Duck is full.
Pippa jumps up.
"Now for a magic surprise!" she yells.
"Sit on the floor
and wait for me."

Pippa runs out
and comes back carrying something.
She calls, "See this beautiful basket
all covered with flowers?
Is it an empty basket?"

Weber Duck waddles over
and puts his bill in Pippa's basket.
"Very empty," he says.

"Yes," says Gray Bird,
looking at the basket
with her bright black eyes.
"It is an empty basket."

Just then, Mother Mouse
hurries out of the room.

"Now shut your eyes tight,"
yells Pippa,
"and turn around three times!"

With eyes shut, everyone turns around
—one, two, three times.

Mother Mouse tiptoes back
into the room.

"Now open your eyes," yells Pippa,
"and look at the magic surprise!"

Everyone looks.
There in the flower basket
is a very pink
very small
very new
baby mouse

blinking its very new eyes.

"Where did you find it, Pippa?"
asks Ripple Squirrel.

"I didn't find it!" shouts Pippa.
"Mother and Father Mouse made it
with mouse magic!
It is our brand-new mouse!
It is a brother mouse for me!"

Everyone stares at the new Brother Mouse.
New Brother Mouse lies still
and blinks and blows baby bubbles.

"But he doesn't talk," says Weber Duck.
"And he doesn't walk," says Gray Bird.
"And he has no fur," says Ripple Squirrel.
"Is he sick?"

Father Mouse laughs.
"No, Brother Mouse is not sick," he says.
"And he will grow fur.
Right now he is just very new.
Now come help celebrate
with wintergreen ice."

"Yes, yes, let's celebrate!"
calls Pippa.

"What does *celebrate* mean?"
whispers Weber Duck.

"It means *eat*," says Ripple.

"Then I will celebrate a lot,"
says Weber.

Everyone sits around the table again
—Gray Bird, Ripple Squirrel,
Weber Duck, Pippa-Squeak,
Cricket, Mother and Father Mouse
—everyone but new Brother Mouse.

"And you know what?" yells Pippa,
waving her spoon in the air.
"Pretty soon Brother Mouse
will walk and talk
and celebrate, too.
And that will be
the best magic trick of all!"

MS READ-a-thon—
a simple way to start youngsters reading

Boys and girls between 6 and 14 can join the MS READ-a-thon and help find a cure for Multiple Sclerosis by reading books. And they get two rewards — the enjoyment of reading, and the great feeling that comes from helping others.

Parents and educators: For complete information call your local MS chapter. Or mail the coupon below.

Kids can help, too!